RAYMOND BRIGGS
Father Christmas goes on Holiday

PUFFIN BOOKS

For Jean

PUFFIN BOOKS

Published by the Penguin Group: London, New York, Australia, Canada,
India, Ireland, New Zealand and South Africa
Penguin Books Ltd, Registered Offices: 80 Strand, London WC2R 0RL, England

puffinbooks.com

First published in Great Britain by Hamish Hamilton 1975
Published in the United States of America by Coward, McCann & Geoghegan 1975
Published in Picture Puffins 1977
Reissued in Puffin Books 1995
038

Copyright © Raymond Briggs, 1975
All rights reserved

The moral right of the author/illustrator has been asserted

Manufactured in China

British Library Cataloguing in Publication Data
A CIP catalogue record for this book is available from the British Library

ISBN: 978-0-140-50187-2

Other books by Raymond Briggs

JIM AND THE BEANSTALK

FATHER CHRISTMAS

FUNGUS THE BOGEYMAN

THE SNOWMAN

THE SNOWMAN STORY BOOK

Father Christmas goes on Holiday

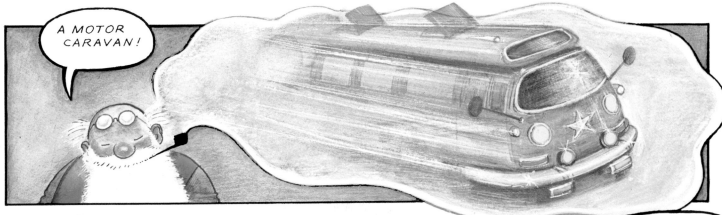

LA BELLE FRANCE!

-ER, BONJOUR, MADEMOISELLE

MADAME! S'IL VOUS PLAIT! BONJOUR, M'SIEUR

OH - ER, PARDON, **MADAME** - ER - JE VEUX ACHETER LE LAIT, S'IL VOUS PLAIT

DU LAIT? OUI, M'SIEUR

MERCI, MADAME!

MERCI, M'SIEUR!

I SPOKE FRENCH! I SPOKE FRENCH!

THIS IS THE LIFE!

OH DEAR, MY TUM!

BAP 748K

THAT NIGHT

NEXT MORNING

CRUMBS! WHAT A NIGHT! NOW THE WHOLE VAN IS ROCKING!

I FEEL SEA-SICK. BETTER GO FOR A WALK

SHOO! SHOO!

BETTER GET TO A PROPER CAMPING GROUND — TOILETS AND EVERYTHING

FACING PAGE, ABOVE: The Queen's round-the-world Commonwealth tour in 1953–4 was the prelude to many more visits to Commonwealth countries which could not be included in that unprecedented inaugural progress. In 1961 Her Majesty and the Duke of Edinburgh spent November and part of December in West Africa. This picture shows a chieftain paying homage to The Queen in Sierra Leone. *(Syndication International)*
FACING PAGE, BELOW LEFT: Her Majesty watches with interest a village craftsman at work in the Gambia. *(Syndication International)*
FACING PAGE, BELOW RIGHT: Since 1953–4

The Queen and the Duke of Edinburgh have made three further visits to New Zealand. The most recent was early in 1974 when they were accompanied by Princess Anne and her husband, Captain Mark Phillips, with whom they are seen here watching a Maori pageant. *(Fox Photos)*
ABOVE: After her visit to the United States in 1976 for the American Bicentennial celebrations, The Queen went to Canada where she opened the Olympic Games. She saw many of the events and was among the first to congratulate the British Modern Pentathlon team who won the first gold medal for Britain.

Prince Edward accompanied his mother when she met the victorious athletes. *(OP & FA)*
BELOW LEFT: Her Majesty is seen arriving to open the Olympic Games in Montreal on 17 July. Immediately behind The Queen are Lord Killanin and other members of the International Olympic Committee. *(OP & FA)*
BELOW RIGHT: The Queen presented the awards at the Commonwealth Games held in Christchurch, New Zealand, in 1974. Judy Vernon of England, winner of the 100-metre hurdles, has just received a gold medal from Her Majesty. *(Syndication International)*

FACING PAGE, TOP: While in Canada in 1976 The Queen and the Duke of Edinburgh gave a banquet on board HMS *Britannia* for the Prime Minister, Pierre Trudeau, and the Governors of all the Provinces of Canada. *(OP & FA)*

FACING PAGE, CENTRE LEFT: The royal launch was escorted by many fascinated spectators at Kuching, Sarawak, during The Queen's tour of South-East Asia and the Indian Ocean in the early part of 1972. *(OP & FA)*

FACING PAGE, CENTRE RIGHT: The Queen watching an official welcoming ceremony by a Maori tribal dancer at Waitangi in the Bay of Islands during her visit to New Zealand in February 1974. A treaty with the natives was signed here in 1840 by a representative of Queen Victoria. *(Fox Photos)*

FACING PAGE, BELOW LEFT: During an overseas tour in March–May 1970 The Queen revisited Australia, this time concentrating on New South Wales, Tasmania, Victoria and Queensland. The picture shows the arrival of Her Majesty and her family at the Henley Stage, Melbourne, Victoria, after sailing by barge up the River Yarra from *Britannia*. *(Keystone)*

FACING PAGE, BELOW RIGHT: The Queen making one of her 'walkabouts' which have so endeared her to the people of many lands. The scene is Kuala Lumpur during the royal visit to South-East Asia in 1972. *(OP & FA)*

ABOVE: During their visit to Canada in the summer of 1973 The Queen and the Duke of Edinburgh were entertained by Red Indian Chief Leonard Pelletier of Fort William, Ontario. *(Popperfoto)*

BELOW LEFT: The Queen waves farewell to London before setting off with the Duke of Edinburgh and Princess Anne for her visit to Canada in July 1970. *(OP & FA)*

BELOW RIGHT: In May 1975, on her way to make her state visit to Japan, The Queen stayed in Hong Kong. During another of her walkabouts she visited a swimming pool in the city and was immediately surrounded by groups of Chinese children who were delighted to welcome her. *(Camera Press)*

Notable and Momentous Events during The Queen's Reign

1952

6 February Death of King George VI. The new Queen recalled from Kenya.
21 February Abolition of identity cards.
5 July Last trams ran in London.
26 July Abdication of King Farouk of Egypt. Death of Eva Peron of Argentina.
15 August Floods in Lynmouth.
23-26 September Visit of King Faisal of Iraq.
29 September John Cobb killed on Loch Ness.
2 October First British atomic weapon exploded.
8 October 112 killed in Harrow rail disaster.
20 October State of emergency in Kenya.
23 October The Queen opened Claerwen Dam.

1953

20 January General Eisenhower sworn in as 34th President of the USA.
1 February Floods on the east coast of England.
5 March Death of Joseph Stalin.
16-21 March Visit by Marshal Tito.
24 March Death of Queen Mary.
24 April Winston Churchill knighted.
29 May Conquest of Mount Everest.
2 June Coronation of Queen Elizabeth II.
15 June Review of the Fleet at Spithead.
23-29 June Coronation visit to Scotland.
1-3 July Coronation visit to Northern Ireland.
9-10 July Coronation visit to Wales.
15 July Coronation review of RAF at Odiham.
27 July Korean armistice agreement signed.
23 November Start of royal Commonwealth tour.

1954

29 April The Queen opened Owen Falls Dam.
6 May Roger Bannister ran first mile in under four minutes.
15 May Royal couple returned to London at end of Commonwealth tour.
28 June-1 July State visit of King of Sweden.
4 July All food rationing ended in Britain.
9 September Earthquake in Algeria.
14-16 October State visit of Haile Selassie.

1955

11 March Death of Sir Alexander Fleming.
5 April Sir Winston Churchill resigned as Premier; succeeded by Sir Anthony Eden.
18 April Death of Albert Einstein.
26 May General election; Tory win.
24-26 June State visit to Norway.
18-23 July Sir Anthony Eden, President Eisenhower, M. Faure and Marshal Bulganin attended Geneva 'Summit' conference.
23 July Donald Campbell set up new world water speed record.
6-9 August Royal visit to Wales and Isle of Man.
22 September ITA service inaugurated.
25-28 October State visit of President of Portugal.
31 October Decision of Princess Margaret not to marry Peter Townsend.
26 November State of emergency in Cyprus.
14 December Mr Gaitskell elected Labour leader, following Mr Atlee's resignation.

1956

28 January-16 February State visit to Nigeria.
19 April Prince Rainier married Grace Kelly.
22 April The Queen received Mr Khrushchev and Marshal Bulganin at Windsor.
8-17 June State visit to Sweden.
3-8 July Royal tour of Scotland.
16-19 July State visits to King of Iraq.
26 July Egypt nationalised Suez Canal.
15 October Duke of Edinburgh started world tour.
17 October The Queen opened Calder Hall nuclear power station.
23 October Hungarian uprising.

1957

10 January Harold Macmillan succeeded as Premier after Anthony Eden's resignation.
18-21 February State visit to Portugal.
8-11 April State visit to Paris.
14 May Petrol rationing ended.
21-25 May State visit to Denmark.
1 June First draw of Premium Bonds.
24-27 July Royal visit to Channel Islands.
12-21 October Royal visits to Canada and USA.
21 October The Queen addressed UN Assembly.
25 December The Queen's Christmas broadcast televised for first time.

1958

31 January First US earth satellite launched.
6 February Eight Manchester United football players killed in Munich air disaster.
2 March Dr Vivian Fuchs completed first crossing of the Antarctic continent.
25-27 March State visit to Netherlands.
13-16 May State visit of Italian President.
1 June De Gaulle became French Premier.
27 June-8 July Royal tour of northern England and Scotland.
14 July Murder of King Faisal of Iraq.
26 July Prince Charles created Prince of Wales.
4 August US submarine *Nautilus* passed under North Pole.
9-11 August Royal visits to Wales and Scotland.
5 October Fifth French Republic began.
9 October Death of Pope Pius XII.
20-23 October State visit of West German President.
28 October Cardinal Roncalli elected Pope. State Opening of Parliament first televised.

1959

1 January Overthrow of Batista regime by Castro.
21 February-3 March Harold Macmillan and Selwyn Lloyd visited Soviet Russia.
5-8 May State visit by Shah of Persia.
18 June-1 August Royal visits to Canada and USA.
26 June The Queen and President Eisenhower formally opened St Lawrence Seaway.
25 July First cross-Channel Hovercraft flight.
8 October General election; Tory win.

1960

19 February Birth of Prince Andrew.
29 February Agadir earthquake, Morocco.
21 March Sharpeville massacre.
5-8 April State visit of President de Gaulle.
1 May US U.2 plane shot down over Russia.
6 May Marriage of Princess Margaret and Antony Armstrong-Jones.
17 May Queen Mother opened Kariba Dam.
30 June Belgian Congo became independent.
4-8 July Visit of Argentinian President.
6 July Death of Aneurin Bevan.
19-20 July State visit of King of Thailand.
5-13 August Royal visits to Wales and Scotland.
10 October The Queen opened new Queen's Bridge at Perth and attended service to mark 400th anniversary of Scottish Reformation.
17-20 October State visit of King of Nepal.
21 October The Queen launched first British nuclear submarine, HMS *Dreadnought*.

1961

20 January John F. Kennedy became US President.
20 January-6 March Royal tour of Cyprus, India, Pakistan, Nepal, Iran and Turkey.
12 April Major Yuri Gagarin of USSR became first astronaut to circle Earth.
2-9 May State visits to Italy and Vatican.
16-18 May Visit of Tunisian President.
17 May Consecration of Guildford Cathedral.
31 May Dr Michael Ramsey succeeded Dr Fisher as Archbishop of Canterbury.
5 June The Queen entertained President Kennedy.
8 June Marriage of Duke of Kent to Miss Katharine Worsley in York Minster.
8 July Angela Mortimer became first English woman holder of Wimbledon title since 1937.
8-9 August Royal visit to Ulster.
13 August East Germany sealed off Berlin border.
17 September UN Secretary-General Dag Hammarskjold killed in African plane crash.
3 November Princess Margaret's son David born.
9 November-6 December Royal visit to West Africa.

1962

6 February-6 April Duke of Edinburgh's tour of South America.
20 February Lt-Col. John Glenn became first American to orbit the Earth.
1 May The Queen attended Silver Wedding celebrations of Queen Juliana.
25 May The Queen attended consecration of Coventry Cathedral.
31 May Adolf Eichmann executed.
26 June Earl of St Andrews born.
3 July Algeria became independent.
10-13 July State visit of Liberian President.
11 July First TV transmission by satellite.
5 August Death of Marilyn Monroe.
16-19 October State visit of King of Norway.
22 October Cuba crisis.

1963

18 January Death of Hugh Gaitskell.
23 January Philby disappeared in Beirut.
31 January-27 March Royal tour of Australasia.
14 February Harold Wilson elected Labour leader.
24 April Princess Alexandra married the Hon. Angus Ogilvy in Westminster Abbey.
14-17 May State visit of King of Belgium.
3 June Death of Pope John XXIII.
12-14 June Visit of President of India.
19 June Valentina Tereshkova of USSR became first woman to orbit the Earth.
21 June Cardinal Montini became Pope.
9-12 July State visit of King of Greece.
26 July Earthquake at Skopje, Yugoslavia.
5 August Nuclear test ban treaty signed.
8 August Great train robbery.
25 September Denning report on Profumo affair.
18 October Harold Macmillan resigned as Premier; succeeded by Earl of Home.
22 November Assassination of President Kennedy; succeeded by Lyndon Johnson.

1964

4-6 January Pope's pilgrimage to Holy Land.
29 February Birth of Princess Alexandra's son James.
10 March Birth of Prince Edward.
28 April Birth of Lady Helen Windsor.
1 May Birth of Lady Sarah Armstrong-Jones.
26-27 May State visit of President of Sudan.
27 May Death of Pandit Nehru.
23-30 June Royal visit to Scotland.
4 September The Queen opened new Forth Bridge.
5-13 October Royal visit to Canada.
15 October General election; Labour win.

1965

4 January Death of T. S. Eliot.
24 January Death of Sir Winston Churchill.
1-12 February State visits to Ethiopia and Sudan.
28 March Death of Princess Royal.
18-28 May State visit to West Germany.
13-15 July State visit of President of Chile.
15 July First close-up pictures of Mars.
22 July Sir Alec Douglas-Home resigned.
27 July Edward Heath elected Tory leader.
4 September Death of Albert Schweitzer.
19 September The Queen unveiled Churchill memorial stone in Westminster Abbey, on 25th anniversary of Battle of Britain.
11 November Rhodesian UDI declared.
16 December Death of Somerset Maugham.

The Royal Portraits

All the portraits in this portfolio are the work of three photographers who have enjoyed recent Royal patronage — Peter Grugeon (the head-and-shoulder studies of The Queen and Prince Philip, the formal portrait of them and the informal family group), Norman Parkinson (Queen Elizabeth the Queen Mother, Princess Anne and Captain Mark Phillips and Princess Margaret and her children), and Carole Cutner (The Prince of Wales).

Peter Grugeon was long established as a portrait photographer specialising in captains of industry and politicians when in 1975 he was invited to submit a portfolio of his work to The Queen. His studies of the Royal Family combine sheer professional brilliance with great charm and naturalness. Peter Grugeon uses an RB 68 6cm x 7cm camera.

Norman Parkinson is one of the world's outstanding photographers of fashion and his expertise in this highly specialised field is apparent in the charming photographs he made of Princess Anne for her 19th and 21st birthdays. Norman Parkinson was also chosen to take the engagement and wedding pictures of Princess Anne and Captain Mark Phillips. Carole Cutner began her photographic career with a box Brownie. She had no formal training in photography and turned professional in 1968. She always works on location, preferring to picture her subjects in their own familiar surroundings. The first photographic appointment with the Prince of Wales came after His Royal Highness had seen the pictures she had taken of him at a dinner given by her daughter's school. Carole Cutner uses Nikon and Hasselblad cameras with a 150mm lens for portraits. Mention must also be made of the press and agency cameramen who follow the Royal progresses. They provided the majority of the photographs in this book, and their contributions are acknowledged in the picture captions.

Notable and Momentous Events during The Queen's Reign

1966
31 January Prince Charles started course at Geelong Grammar School, Melbourne.
1 February–5 March Royal tour of Caribbean.
31 March General election; Labour win.
9–13 May State visit to Belgium.
15 May–1 July Seamen's strike.
17–18 May State visit of Austrian President.
4 July Royal visit to Belfast.
19–21 July State visit of King of Jordan.
30 July England won World Cup.
31 July Princess Alexandra's daughter born.
27 August Francis Chichester started single-handed round-the-world voyage.
6 September Assassination of Dr Verwoerd.
8 September The Queen opened Severn Bridge.
21 October Aberfan disaster.
28 October Abolition of capital punishment.
4 November Severe floods in Florence.
17–29 November Visit of President of Pakistan.
2 December Tiger talks on Rhodesia.

1967
9 February The Queen entertained Mr Kosygin.
19 March The tanker *Torrey Canyon* ran aground.
21 April Military coup in Greece.
9–17 May State visit of King of Saudi Arabia.
30 May Biafra declared its secession.
5–10 June Six-day war in Middle East.
30 June–5 July Royal tour of Canada on centenary of Canada's confederation.
20 September The Queen launched liner *Queen Elizabeth II* at Clydebank.
8 October Death of Earl Attlee.
Prince Charles entered Trinity College, Cambridge.
19 October The Queen opened new Tyne Tunnel.
25 October Visit of West German Chancellor.
1–4 November State visit of Turkish President.
14–17 November Royal visit to Malta.
3 December First human heart transplant.

1968
1 April The Queen attended RAF 50th anniversary banquet at Lancaster House.
4 April Martin Luther King assassinated.
24–27 April State visit by Danish King.
2 May The Queen attended Oxford Union debate.
29 May Manchester United won European Cup.
5 June Robert Kennedy assassinated.
17 June Prince Charles made Knight of Garter.
10 July Yachtsman Alec Rose knighted.
29 July Visit of President of Pakistan.
20 August Russian invasion of Czechoslovakia.
27 August Death of Princess Marina.
1–18 November State visits to Brazil and Chile.

1969
4 February The Queen received American spaceman Frank Borman.
25 February President Nixon lunched with The Queen.
28 March Death of General Eisenhower.
9 April British Concorde's maiden flight.
20 April Prince Charles began term at University of Wales, Aberystwyth.
22–30 April State visit by Italian President.
28 April President de Gaulle resigned.
5–10 May State visit to Austria.
19 May The Queen opened General Assembly of Church of Scotland.
15 June M. Pompidou elected French President.
1 July Investiture of Prince of Wales.
15–20 July State visit by President of Finland.
20 July First men landed on the Moon.
14 October The Queen received *Apollo 11* crew.
14 November 21st birthday of Prince Charles.
5 December Death of Princess Andrew of Greece.

1970
25 January End of Nigerian civil war.
1 February Death of Bertrand Russell.
11 February Duke of Edinburgh left to visit Cape Kennedy space launching centre. Prince Charles took seat in Lords.
3 March–3 May Royal visit to Australasia.
31 May Earthquake in Peru.
18 June General election; Conservative win.
5–16 July Royal visit to Canada.
16–20 July Prince Charles and Princess Anne stayed at the White House.
25 July Duchess of Kent's son Nicholas born.
28 September Death of President Nasser.
9 November Death of General de Gaulle.

1971
20 January–7 March Post Office strike.
2 February Duke of Edinburgh started tour of Pacific Islands and Australia.
15 February Decimal coinage introduced.
26 March Civil war in Pakistan.
6 April Death of Stravinsky.
3–12 May Royal visit to British Columbia.
24 June The Queen opened second Mersey Tunnel.
28 July Prince of Wales made parachute jump into English Channel.
5 August Industrial Relations Act passed.
15 August 21st birthday of Princess Anne.
5 September Princess Anne won individual championship at European Horse Trials.
5–8 October State visit of Emperor Hirohito.
18–25 October State visit to Turkey.
7–9 December State visit of King of Afghanistan.
17 December End of Indo-Pakistan war and formation of Bangladesh.

1972
9 January–27 February National miners' strike.
22 January Mr Heath signed Treaty of Accession for British entry into EEC.
30 January 'Bloody Sunday' in Londonderry. Pakistan left Commonwealth.
9 February–26 March Royal visit to South-East Asia and Indian Ocean.
21–28 February President Nixon's visit to China.
30 March Direct rule for Northern Ireland.
11–14 April State visit of Dutch Queen.
15–19 May State visit to France.
28 May Death of Duke of Windsor in Paris.
13–15 June State visit of Grand Duke of Luxembourg.
8 July Wedding of Prince Richard of Gloucester to Miss Birgitte van Deurs.
9 August Amin expelled Asians.
28 August Prince William killed in air crash.
5 September Massacre at Munich Olympics.
17–21 October State visit to Yugoslavia.
24–27 October State visit of West German President.
20 November Silver wedding anniversary of The Queen and the Duke of Edinburgh.

1973
23 January Vietnam cease-fire agreement.
9–25 February Princess Anne visited Ethiopia and Sudan.
8 March Bombs in London marked Ulster border poll.
26 March Death of Noël Coward.
3–6 April State visit of Mexican President.
8 April Death of Picasso.
11–15 June State visit of General Gowon.
25 June–6 July Royal visit to Canada.
11 September Overthrow of Allende in Chile.
1 October Start of Arab-Israeli war.
15–23 October Royal tour of Australia.
13 November State of emergency declared after overtime ban by electricity and coal workers.
14 November Marriage of Princess Anne to Captain Mark Phillips.
11–14 December State visit of President of Zaire.
18 December Car bombs in London.

1974
7 January Beginning of 'Three-day Week'.
27 January–28 February Royal tour of Pacific Islands and Australasia.
28 February General election.
4 March Edward Heath resigned; new minority government formed by Wilson.
18–23 March State visit to Indonesia.
20 March Princess Anne ambushed in Mall.
30 April–3 May State visit of Queen of Denmark.
19 May M. Giscard d'Estaing elected French President.
1 June Flixborough chemical plant explosion.
10 June Death of Duke of Gloucester.
13 June Prince Charles' maiden speech in Lords.
9–12 July State visit of King of Malaysia.
15 July Overthrow of President Makarios.
20 July Turkish invasion of Cyprus.
23 July Greek colonels relinquished power.
8 August President Nixon resigned after Watergate scandal; President Ford succeeded.
10 October General election; Labour win.
24 October Birth of Earl of Ulster.
21 November Birmingham pubs bombed.

1975
31 January Death of Duke of Norfolk.
11 February Mrs Thatcher elected Tory leader.
16 February–2 March Royal visit to Caribbean and Mexico.
28 February Moorgate train disaster.
25 March King Faisal assassinated.
13 April Start of civil war in Lebanon.
26–30 April Royal visit to Jamaica.
4–12 May Royal visits to Hong Kong and Japan.
5 June Suez canal re-opened.
Referendum on EEC.
26 June State of emergency in India.
8–11 July State visit of King of Sweden.
17 July First US-Soviet space link-up.
1–3 August State visit of President of Guyana.
27 August Death of Haile Selassie.
3 November The Queen inaugurated Forties oil field.
11 November Mr Whitlam dismissed by Australian Governor-General.
12 November Sex Discrimination Bill enacted.
18–21 November State visit of Tanzanian President.
20 November General Franco died.

1976
8 January Death of Chou En-lai.
4 February Earthquake in Guatemala City.
11 February OAU recognised new Angolan republic.
19 February Iceland severed diplomatic relations with Britain.
16 March Mr Wilson announced resignation.
19 March Separation of Princess Margaret and Lord Snowdon.
5 April James Callaghan became Premier.
27 April Trial of John Stonehouse began.
4–7 May Visit of President of Brazil.
24–28 May State visit to Finland.
16–24 June 176 killed in South African township riots.
22–25 June State visit of French President.
3–4 July Israeli raid at Entebbe airport.
6–26 July Royal visits to USA and Canada.
7 July David Steel elected Liberal leader.
21 July British ambassador to Eire murdered.
28 July Diplomatic relations with Uganda severed.
9 September Death of Mao Tse-tung.
8–10 November State visit to Luxembourg.
4 December Death of Benjamin Britten.

1977
14 January Death of Lord Avon.
20 January Jimmy Carter sworn in as 39th President of the USA.
9 February–31 March Royal Jubilee Tour of Australasia.

Queen of the United Kingdom

Although not one year of The Queen's reign has gone by when she did not make visits abroad, Her Majesty has also fulfilled a demanding programme at home and furthermore, to the pleasure of the nation, given birth to two more princes. Prince Andrew was born on 19 February 1960 and Prince Edward on 10 March 1964. Their brother Charles, the heir apparent, was already Prince of Wales, a title at the bestowal of the Sovereign. He was so created on 26 July 1958, the announcement being recorded by The Queen, who was ill, and introduced by the Duke of Edinburgh at the close of the Commonwealth and Empire

Continued on page 20

TOP: On 19 May 1969 The Queen opened the General Assembly of the Church of Scotland, the first time that a reigning monarch has done so since the Reformation. The setting was the Assembly Hall in Edinburgh. (*Fox Photos*)

ABOVE LEFT: The Service of Remembrance for the dead of the two World Wars is held every year at the Cenotaph in Whitehall on the Sunday nearest to 11 November, the Armistice Day of World War I. Traditionally, the Sovereign lays the first wreath of poppies, followed by other members of the Royal Family, political party leaders and heads of the armed services. (*OP & FA*)

ABOVE RIGHT: The Queen leaving Rochester Cathedral after the Office for the Royal Maundy in 1961. Every year on the Thursday of Holy Week the Sovereign or another member of the Royal Family distributes the specially minted Maundy Money to elderly people: traditionally, since 1890, at Westminster Abbey, but since Her Majesty's accession at various other cathedral churches. (*OP & FA*)

FACING PAGE: The Investiture of Prince Charles as Prince of Wales at Caernarvon Castle on 1 July 1969. The Queen is seen here receiving her son's homage after she had placed the jewelled coronet on his head. (*Keystone*)

Games at Cardiff. On 1 July 1969, in an enchanting ceremony on the lawns of Caernarvon Castle, where the first English Prince of Wales was born in 1284, The Queen crowned her son with a jewelled coronet and invested him with his robe of purple velvet and ermine. Apart from unique occasions such as this, The Queen's public engagements take her to every part of the United Kingdom, a pattern of progresses established at the start of her reign, when she began by visiting Scotland, Wales and Northern Ireland. Reviews, visits to hospitals, industrial works and mines, schools and welfare organisations, the opening of new buildings, attendance at a film or stage *première* or the Cup Final of the Football Association, all these and many other activities come within The Queen's varied range: but basically Her Majesty's calendar is planned according to precedent. The service for the Distribution of the Royal Maundy, one of the most ancient ceremonies in the Christian Church, is observed annually. Choosing a different cathedral or abbey church each year, Her Majesty presents the specially minted Maundy Money and other gifts to elderly men and women, whose number corresponds with the years of

Continued on page 22

* * *

TOP LEFT: The Queen carries out many formal engagements on her visits to Scotland. Here Her Majesty is inspecting a guard of honour on her arrival in the Highlands. *(OP & FA)*

FACING PAGE, TOP RIGHT: The Queen chats with one of the Chelsea Pensioners during her visit to the Royal Hospital, Chelsea, as Inspecting Officer of the Founder's Day Parade, 29 May 1962. (*Syndication International*)

FACING PAGE, CENTRE RIGHT: In July 1966 The Queen and the Duke of Edinburgh visited Northern Ireland and were entertained by the Lord Mayor of Belfast. (*Syndication International*)

FACING PAGE, BELOW: Each year The Queen's summer season ends with a series of garden parties at Buckingham Palace. Many of the guests are presented to Her Majesty as she walks through the grounds. (*OP & FA*)

TOP LEFT: The Queen donned protective clothing for her visit to the Westfield open-cast site in Fife on 27 June 1961. (*OP & FA*)

TOP RIGHT: When Her Majesty opened the new London Bridge in 1973 she arrived in the Port of London Authority launch *Nore*. (*Fox Photos*)

ABOVE: The Queen and the Duke of Edinburgh, in the robes of the Order of the British Empire, are seen arriving for a service in the OBE Chapel in St Paul's Cathedral. (*OP & FA*)

RIGHT: As Sovereign, The Queen is commander-in-chief of all the armed forces of the Crown and in this capacity reviews the Home Fleet. Her Majesty is inspecting the crew of HMS *Dido* while attending the review in the Firth of Clyde in 1965. (*Syndication International*)

her age. In accordance with custom, the court removes from Buckingham Palace to Windsor Castle for Easter and Royal Ascot Race Week, Her Majesty being then 'in residence' at this most ancient of royal palaces. After holding the Garter Ceremony on Monday of Ascot Week, The Queen and Royal Family attend the Royal Ascot Race Meetings on the following four days, driving in cars to a point in Windsor Great Park where they change into open carriages for the traditional drive up the course. The Queen's annual residence at the Palace of Holyroodhouse in Edinburgh, third of the official royal homes, inherited from the Scottish house of Stuart which in the person of James I succeeded to the English throne in 1603, usually takes place in July. The year ends on a note of warmth and intimacy with Her

Majesty's Christmas Day broadcast, in which she continues a practice begun by King George V in 1932. Since 1957 the broadcast has been televised, so bringing the greater realism projected by a medium which immeasurably heightens, on this as on so many other occasions, the human understanding between the monarchy and the world.

   ★   ★   ★

ABOVE LEFT: Her Majesty meets Coco, one of the most famous and popular clowns in history, on a visit to a special performance of Bertram Mills Circus in 1965. *(Fox Photos)*
ABOVE CENTRE: Britain's National Theatre was at last a reality when The Queen arrived for the official opening on 25 October 1976. *(Keystone)*
ABOVE RIGHT: Her Majesty presenting the Football Association Cup to Peter Rod-

rigues, captain of Southampton, who beat Manchester United 1-0 in the 1976 Cup Final. *(Owen Barnes)*
BELOW: The traditional introduction to each day's race meeting at Royal Ascot in June is the royal procession up the course to the Royal Enclosure. Unless the weather is particularly unkind, The Queen and other members of the Royal Family arrive in open landaus. The Royal Ascot is the race meeting most closely associated with the Crown. Queen Anne first visited the course in 1711 and up to recent times it was used for only four days' racing each year. In 1946 King George VI agreed that there should be a number of extra days and with National Hunt meetings there are now 23 days' racing. The Queen's Representative at Ascot is the Marquess of Abergavenny. *(OP & FA)*

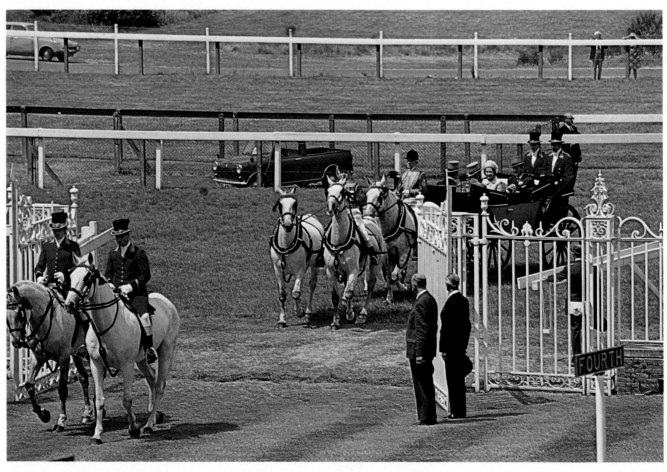

Royal Ambassador

The Queen has so far during her reign made thirty state visits to foreign countries, more than any previous sovereign and to these can be added a comparable number of private visits abroad. On her state visits, as on Commonwealth tours, The Queen has been accompanied by the Duke of Edinburgh. The first after her accession was to King Haakon VII of Norway in 1955. The following year she went to Sweden. In 1957 she made four state visits: to Portugal, France, Denmark and (after opening the Canadian Parliament) the United States of America. When in 1958 Her Majesty paid a state visit to Queen Juliana of the Netherlands she appointed Queen Juliana a Lady of the Garter, a dignity shared by that sovereign lady with her mother, Princess (formerly Queen) Wilhelmina, and our own Queen Elizabeth the Queen Mother. The year 1961 was exceptionally busy, as interlinked with the Commonwealth tour of India and Pakistan there were state visits to Nepal and Iran, and subsequent state visits

were made in May to Italy and to His Holiness Pope John at the Vatican City, and to Liberia in November. State visits followed in 1965 to Ethiopia and the Sudan and later West Germany, where from 18–28 May the route of fifteen stages ranged from Bonn to Berlin and Hanover, the last a place of special significance for Her Majesty. From Hanover in 1714 the Elector Georg Ludwig came to England to reign as George I, securing the Protestant succession through his mother, the Electress Sophie, granddaughter of James I. Further state visits were made to Belgium in 1966, Brazil and Chile in 1968, Austria in 1969, Turkey in 1971, Thailand, the Maldives, France and Yugoslavia in 1972, Indonesia in 1974, Mexico and Japan in 1975, and in 1976 Finland, the United States of America and Luxembourg. This second state visit to the United States, before Her Majesty went to Canada to open the Olympic Games, marked the Bicentenary of the Declaration of Independence and took her to

Philadelphia, Washington, New York, Boston and Charlottesville, a city which commemorates America's last Queen, Charlotte, consort of George III, from whom Elizabeth II has a double descent. Her Majesty is indeed in her sincerity and strict sense of vocation remarkably like the fair-haired Princess of Mecklenburg-Strelitz who, at the age of 17, married George III on the evening of her arrival in England, never having met him before, and after years of happiness remained during his tragic illness an exemplary wife and queen. Elizabeth II, strikingly poised and beautiful in her early maturity, entranced America. The discord of loyalties long ago found repose in the

Continued on page 24

*   *   *

ABOVE: A glittering and gracious figure, The Queen arrives at a banquet during her state visit to Thailand which formed part of the royal tour of South-East Asia in February and March 1972. *(OP & FA)*

presence of this most accomplished and tireless of royal ambassadors. An American lady, writing to a friend in England after the state reception at the White House in Washington, spoke of her as 'our present Queen' and said, 'She looked like a tranquil dream . . . All Americans cannot help loving the Sovereign of dear England.' Her Majesty and the Duke of Edinburgh were accorded a warmly demonstrative welcome also when in November 1976 they paid a state visit to Luxembourg as guests of the Grand Duke Jean and the Grand Duchess Joséphine-Charlotte. Although this was the first visit of a reigning British monarch to the Grand Duchy, there have been close ties since the seventh century, when the Northumbrian-born patron saint of Luxembourg, Willibrord, converted the country to Christianity. Her Majesty concluded her official programme with a visit to St Willibrord's tomb at Echternach.

Continued on page 26

★　　★　　★

TOP LEFT: The Queen and the Duke of Edinburgh have made a great many impressive state visits, but none filled with more colourful and novel experiences than the one to India, Pakistan, Nepal and Iran in 1961. Riding on elephants, Her Majesty and the Duke accompanied the Royal Family of Nepal into tiger country. (*Popperfoto*)

TOP RIGHT: The Queen, with the Duke of Edinburgh and Princess Anne, enjoyed another unusual mode of travel during their visit to Thailand in the early part of 1972. (*OP & FA*)

FACING PAGE, CENTRE RIGHT: In May 1976 The Queen and the Duke of Edinburgh voyaged through northern waters on a state visit to 'the land of a thousand lakes', Finland. The royal yacht *Britannia* docked at Helsinki, where they were received by President Kekkonen. *(OP & FA)*

FACING PAGE, BELOW LEFT: When in August 1969 The Queen and her family sailed in *Britannia* to pay a private visit to Norway they were met at sea by King Olav. They later came ashore in the royal barge for a dinner party with members of the Norwegian Royal Family. *(Syndication International)*

ABOVE LEFT: The Queen is the first reigning British monarch to have visited Japan. Her Majesty and the Duke of Edinburgh made a state visit in May 1975 as guests of Emperor Hirohito and Empress Nagako, with whom they are seen in this picture. They went to Tokyo, Kyoto and Toba. *(OP & FA)*

ABOVE RIGHT: When in May 1961 The Queen and the Duke of Edinburgh made a state visit to Naples and Rome, Her Majesty wore for her meeting with Pope John XXIII at the Vatican the traditional long black gown, with pearls given her by Queen Mary and a tiara which had belonged to Queen Alexandra. *(Fox Photos)*

RIGHT: In May 1965 The Queen and her consort made a state visit to West Germany. Their many engagements included a dinner party in Bonn given for President Lubke and his wife. *(Fox Photos)*

Her lengthy experience of other countries began before her accession. With Princess Margaret she accompanied The King and Queen in 1947 to South Africa, where she celebrated her 21st birthday. As Queen she first set foot on foreign soil on Sunday 29 November 1953, when she landed at Panama in the course of her Commonwealth world tour. A private visit to Denmark in 1960 gave her the opportunity to become still better acquainted with the native land of her beautiful great-grandmother, Queen Alexandra, whose second brother, Prince William, became King George I of Greece and grandfather of the Duke of Edinburgh (His Royal Highness is thus related to The Queen by Danish as well as English descent). A visit to France on 16 June 1974 brought Her Majesty the personal pleasure of seeing her filly, Highclere, win the Prix de Diane at Chantilly.

*　　　*　　　*

TOP LEFT: Although the state visit to Yugoslavia in October 1972 was the first made by a reigning British monarch to a Communist country, it did not lack mutual interest as President Tito, seen with Her Majesty in this happy photograph, was acquainted with England, where he had been shown over Windsor Castle some years earlier. *(OP & FA)*
CENTRE LEFT: On 18 October 1971 The Queen, with the Duke and Princess Anne, arrived at Ankara to pay a state visit to Turkey. From the airport they drove through the streets of the city and in the evening were entertained at a banquet given by the President and Mrs Sunay. During their seven-day visit The Queen and her family visited Istanbul, Kemal Ataturk's tomb, the ruins at Ephesus and the Gallipoli battlefields. *(OP & FA)*

26

FACING PAGE, BELOW LEFT: The Duke of Edinburgh, who had left England in October 1956 on a four-month world tour, was reunited with The Queen in Portugal, where Her Majesty arrived by air on 16 February 1957 to begin a state visit planned to include Lisbon, Oporto and a 200-mile drive through the countryside. On 22 February, the day after their return home, the Duke was accorded the style 'Prince of the United Kingdom'. *(OP & FA)*

FACING PAGE, RIGHT: The people of the United States expressed in heart-warming ways their appreciation of The Queen's state visit for the Bicentennial celebrations in 1976. In Washington, where Her Majesty and the Duke of Edinburgh were welcomed by President and Mrs Ford, the grand round of ceremonies allowed time for sightseeing and Her Majesty visited several monuments including those on Capitol Hill. *(OP & FA)*

TOP: President Ford gave a ball at the White House in honour of his royal visitors, and in the picture on the left he is dancing with The Queen. *(OP & FA)*

CENTRE RIGHT: At Boston, scene in 1773 of the 'Boston Tea Party' which flouted British rule and foreshadowed the revolutionary war, very different sentiments prevailed in 1976, as The Queen saw with smiling pleasure. *(OP & FA)*

BELOW RIGHT: In May 1972 The Queen and the Duke paid a five-day state visit to France. They were met at Orly Airport by President and Madame Pompidou. While in Paris Her Majesty called on the Duke and Duchess of Windsor at their home: it was the last time she saw her uncle, who died a few days later. The royal programme included visits to Versailles, Nîmes, Arles, Avignon and Rouen. *(Camera Press)*

27

The Queen and Her Family

As Princess Elizabeth The Queen spent much of her life amid the green miles of Windsor Great Park. There the Duke and Duchess of York had as their country home The Royal Lodge, originally a thatched cottage built by George IV, which is separated from Windsor Castle by the three-mile avenue of the Long Walk. The Queen's love of horse-riding dates from those early years. When her father became King she and Princess Margaret found other sources of pleasure in the Home Park Private around the castle, and especially at Frogmore, an enclosure of lake and lawns within the Home Park Private. At the south-west corner of Frogmore stands the mausoleum of Queen Victoria and Albert, Prince Consort, and beside it the private royal cemetery, but there is no sense of morbidity: at the north-east is Queen Charlotte's cream-walled house, over-looking her ornamental lake used by younger members of the modern Royal Family for boating. Frogmore was Queen Charlotte's 'bijou', bought by her for her botanical studies, and eventually became, in accordance with a desire implied in her will, 'an Appendage to Windsor Castle'. Together with her farm, Shaw Farm, it considerably enlarged the Home Park Private, creating outdoor amenities which were one reason for the present

Queen's increased use of the castle. Although Buckingham Palace remains the capital residence, The Queen enter-tains visiting royalty and heads of state at Windsor, the royal family Christmas house-party forgathers there, and when-ever possible The Queen goes to Windsor to ride and exercise her dogs at weekends. It happens that the bicentenary of the use of Queen's Tower, which commands panoramic views at the south-east corner of the castle, as the private suite of the Queens of England coincides with the Jubilee Year: it was in 1777 that Queen Charlotte first chose it for that purpose and every succeeding Queen has lived there. With so much to offer, only twenty-five miles from London, Windsor was bound to win the affection of a young and versatile royal family. The equestrian prowess and courage of Princess Anne, who on 14 November 1973 married Captain Mark Phillips, were bred there. Popular enjoyment, stimulated by royal patronage, centres on Windsor Horse Show, held yearly in the Home Park Public on the north side of the castle, and polo on Smith's Lawn in the Great Park, in which the Duke of Edinburgh and the Prince of Wales often take part. Sharing her heritage still further with the world, The Queen annually opens Frogmore Gardens to the

ABOVE: This picture of the Royal Couple at Balmoral was specially taken for the Silver Jubilee. *(Keystone)*
FACING PAGE, TOP LEFT: The Queen and members of the Royal Family being pre-sented with bouquets of heather at the Braemar Games in Scotland. *(OP & FA)*
FACING PAGE, TOP RIGHT: The Queen, with Prince Charles and Princess Anne, at the Royal Windsor Horse Show in 1956. *(OP & FA)*
FACING PAGE, CENTRE AND RIGHT: The Queen and her family inherit their Scottish blood and love of the Highlands from the Queen Mother, and also from their remoter ancestors the Stuart kings. Woods and meads and mountains, the sparkling river, the royal Highland cattle, all blend at Balmoral into an environment which, as the four pictures opposite show, offers the perfect royal holiday retreat: yet as a sovereign home Balmoral is quite modern and was the choice of a German-born prince, Albert, Prince Consort, who bought the estate in 1852 and personally planned the present castle and grounds. The Gaelic name means 'the majestic dwelling'. To Queen Victoria, Balmoral was 'this dear Paradise'. *(Camera Press, Fox Photos & Focus Four)*
FACING PAGE, BELOW LEFT: The Queen and her family in Bromont, Canada, at the end of her state visit in 1976. *(OP & FA)*

28

Continued on page 30

12. Which one of the following is true for the function g where $g'(x) = x^2 + 2x + 1$?

    A g is never increasing.

    B g is decreasing then increasing.

    C g is increasing then decreasing.

    D g is never decreasing.

13. Simplify $\log_2(x + 1) - 2\log_2 3$.

    A $\log_2\left(\dfrac{x+1}{9}\right)$

    B $\log_2(x - 8)$

    C $\log_2(x - 2)$

    D $\log_2 6(x + 1)$

14. The diagram shows the graph of $y = g(x)$.

Which diagram below shows the graph of $y = 3 - g(x)$?

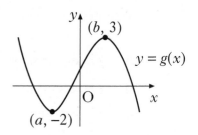

A

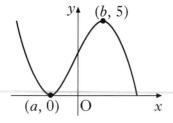

B

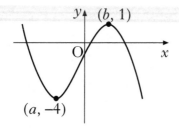

C

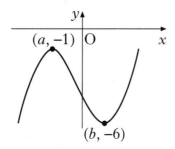

D

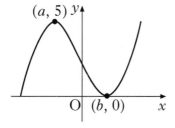

15. Points P and Q have coordinates (1, 3, −1) and (2, 5, 1) and T is the midpoint of PQ.

What is the position vector of T?

A $\begin{pmatrix} -\dfrac{3}{2} \\ -4 \\ 0 \end{pmatrix}$

B $\begin{pmatrix} \dfrac{3}{2} \\ 4 \\ 0 \end{pmatrix}$

C $\begin{pmatrix} -\dfrac{1}{2} \\ -1 \\ -1 \end{pmatrix}$

D $\begin{pmatrix} -1 \\ -2 \\ -2 \end{pmatrix}$

16. A = (−3, 4, 7) and B = (−1, 8, 3).

If $\overrightarrow{AD} = 4\overrightarrow{AB}$, what are the coordinates of D?

A (−9, −8, −13)

B (5, −4, 1)

C (−6, 8, 14)

D (5, 20, −9)

17. The equation of the parabola shown is of the form $y = kx(x - 6)$.

What is the value of k?

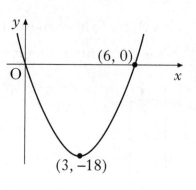

A 0

B $\dfrac{1}{144}$

C 2

D 6

18. Given that $y = 3\cos 5x$, find $\dfrac{dy}{dx}$.

A $15\cos 5x$

B $-15\sin 5x$

C $-15\cos x$

D $3\cos 5$

19. Find $\displaystyle\int (4x+1)^{\frac{1}{2}} \, dx$.

A $\dfrac{1}{6}(4x+1)^{\frac{3}{2}} + c$

B $\dfrac{1}{4}(4x+1) + c$

C $\dfrac{1}{4}(4x+1)^{\frac{3}{2}} + c$

D $2(4x+1)^{-\frac{3}{2}} + c$

20. Given that $\int (3x+1)^{-\frac{1}{2}}\, dx = \frac{2}{3}(3x+1)^{\frac{1}{2}} + c$, find $\int_0^1 (3x+1)^{-\frac{1}{2}}\, dx.$

A $\dfrac{2}{3}$

B $\dfrac{4}{3}$

C   2

D $\sqrt{2}$

[END OF SECTION A]

ALL questions should be attempted.

Marks

1. Find the coordinates of the turning points of the curve with equation $y = x^3 - 3x^2 - 9x + 12$ and determine their nature.

   8

2. Functions f and g are given by $f(x) = 3x + 1$ and $g(x) = x^2 - 2$.

   (a) (i) Find $p(x)$ where $p(x) = f(g(x))$.

        (ii) Find $q(x)$ where $q(x) = g(f(x))$.

        3

   (b) Solve $p'(x) = q'(x)$.

        3

3. (a) (i) Show that $x = 1$ is a root of $x^3 + 8x^2 + 11x - 20 = 0$.

        (ii) Hence factorise $x^3 + 8x^2 + 11x - 20$ fully.

        4

   (b) Solve $\log_2(x + 3) + \log_2(x^2 + 5x - 4) = 3$.

        5

4. (a) Show that the point $P(5, 10)$ lies on circle C_1 with equation $(x + 1)^2 + (y - 2)^2 = 100$.

        1

   (b) PQ is a diameter of this circle as shown in the diagram. Find the equation of the tangent at Q.

        5

   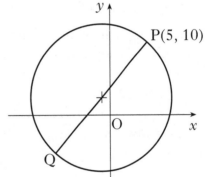

   (c) Two circles, C_2 and C_3, touch circle C_1 at Q.

   The radius of each of these circles is twice the radius of circle C_1.

   Find the equations of circles C_2 and C_3.

        4

   [Turn over

Marks

5. The graphs of $y = f(x)$ and $y = g(x)$ are shown in the diagram.

   $f(x) = -4\cos(2x) + 3$ and $g(x)$ is of the form $g(x) = m\cos(nx)$.

   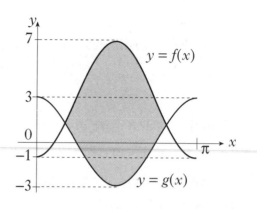

   (a) Write down the values of m and n.   **1**

   (b) Find, correct to one decimal place, the coordinates of the points of intersection of the two graphs in the interval $0 \le x \le \pi$.   **5**

   (c) Calculate the shaded area.   **6**

6. The size of the human population, N, can be modelled using the equation $N = N_0 e^{rt}$ where N_0 is the population in 2006, t is the time in years since 2006, and r is the annual rate of increase in the population.

   (a) In 2006 the population of the United Kingdom was approximately 61 million, with an annual rate of increase of 1·6%. Assuming this growth rate remains constant, what would be the population in 2020?   **2**

   (b) In 2006 the population of Scotland was approximately 5·1 million, with an annual rate of increase of 0·43%.

   Assuming this growth rate remains constant, how long would it take for Scotland's population to double in size?   **3**

7. Vectors p, q and r are represented on the diagram shown where angle ADC $= 30°$.

   It is also given that $|p| = 4$ and $|q| = 3$.

   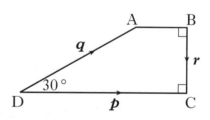

   (a) Evaluate $p.(q + r)$ and $r.(p - q)$.   **6**

   (b) Find $|q + r|$ and $|p - q|$.   **4**

[END OF QUESTION PAPER]

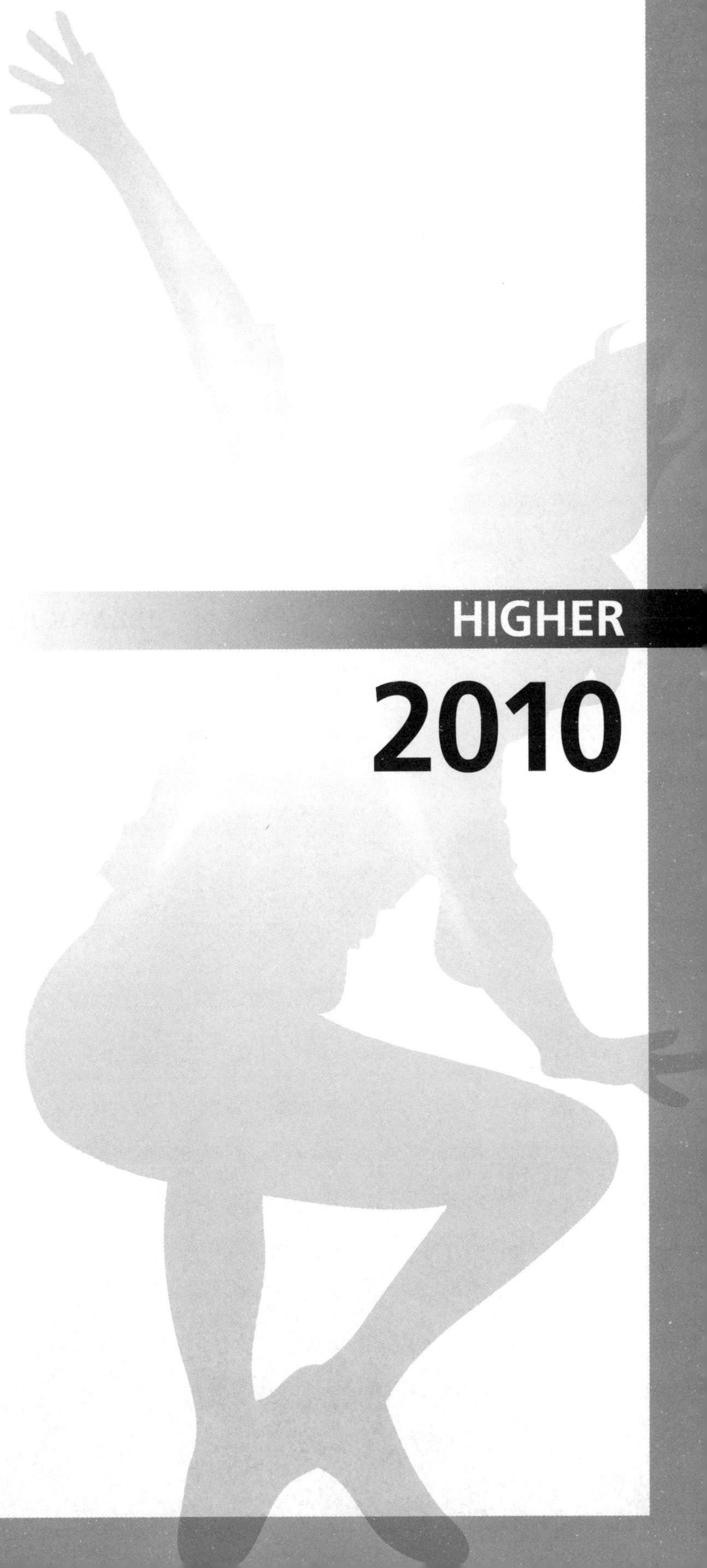

HIGHER

2010

X100/301

NATIONAL
QUALIFICATIONS
2011

WEDNESDAY, 18 MAY
9.00 AM – 10.30 AM

MATHEMATICS
HIGHER
Paper 1
(Non-calculator)

Read carefully

Calculators may NOT be used in this paper.

Section A – Questions 1–20 (40 marks)

Instructions for completion of **Section A** are given on page two.

For this section of the examination you must use an **HB pencil**.

Section B (30 marks)

1   Full credit will be given only where the solution contains appropriate working.

2   Answers obtained by readings from scale drawings will not receive any credit.

Read carefully

1　Check that the answer sheet provided is for **Mathematics Higher (Section A)**.

2　For this section of the examination you must use an **HB pencil** and, where necessary, an eraser.

3　Check that the answer sheet you have been given has **your name**, **date of birth**, **SCN** (Scottish Candidate Number) and **Centre Name** printed on it.

　Do not change any of these details.

4　If any of this information is wrong, tell the Invigilator immediately.

5　If this information is correct, **print** your name and seat number in the boxes provided.

6　The answer to each question is **either** A, B, C or D. Decide what your answer is, then, using your pencil, put a horizontal line in the space provided (see sample question below).

7　There is **only one correct** answer to each question.

8　Rough working should **not** be done on your answer sheet.

9　At the end of the exam, put the **answer sheet for Section A inside the front cover of your answer book**.

Sample Question

A curve has equation $y = x^3 - 4x$.

What is the gradient at the point where $x = 2$?

　　A　8

　　B　1

　　C　0

　　D　−4

The correct answer is **A**—8. The answer **A** has been clearly marked in **pencil** with a horizontal line (see below).

Changing an answer

If you decide to change your answer, carefully erase your first answer and, using your pencil, fill in the answer you want. The answer below has been changed to **D**.

FORMULAE LIST

Circle:

The equation $x^2 + y^2 + 2gx + 2fy + c = 0$ represents a circle centre $(-g, -f)$ and radius $\sqrt{g^2 + f^2 - c}$.

The equation $(x - a)^2 + (y - b)^2 = r^2$ represents a circle centre (a, b) and radius r.

Scalar Product: $\mathbf{a}.\mathbf{b} = |\mathbf{a}|\,|\mathbf{b}|\cos\theta$, where θ is the angle between $\mathbf{a}$ and $\mathbf{b}$

or $\mathbf{a}.\mathbf{b} = a_1b_1 + a_2b_2 + a_3b_3$ where $\mathbf{a} = \begin{pmatrix} a_1 \\ a_2 \\ a_3 \end{pmatrix}$ and $\mathbf{b} = \begin{pmatrix} b_1 \\ b_2 \\ b_3 \end{pmatrix}$.

Trigonometric formulae:

$$\sin(A \pm B) = \sin A \cos B \pm \cos A \sin B$$
$$\cos(A \pm B) = \cos A \cos B \mp \sin A \sin B$$
$$\sin 2A = 2\sin A \cos A$$
$$\cos 2A = \cos^2 A - \sin^2 A$$
$$= 2\cos^2 A - 1$$
$$= 1 - 2\sin^2 A$$

Table of standard derivatives:

$f(x)$	$f'(x)$
$\sin ax$	$a\cos ax$
$\cos ax$	$-a\sin ax$

Table of standard integrals:

$f(x)$	$\int f(x)\,dx$
$\sin ax$	$-\dfrac{1}{a}\cos ax + C$
$\cos ax$	$\dfrac{1}{a}\sin ax + C$

[Turn over

SECTION A

ALL questions should be attempted.

1. Given that $\mathbf{p} = \begin{pmatrix} 2 \\ 5 \\ -7 \end{pmatrix}$, $\mathbf{q} = \begin{pmatrix} 1 \\ 0 \\ -1 \end{pmatrix}$ and $\mathbf{r} = \begin{pmatrix} -4 \\ 2 \\ 0 \end{pmatrix}$, express $2\mathbf{p} - \mathbf{q} - \frac{1}{2}\mathbf{r}$ in component form.

A $\begin{pmatrix} 1 \\ 9 \\ -15 \end{pmatrix}$

B $\begin{pmatrix} 1 \\ 11 \\ -13 \end{pmatrix}$

C $\begin{pmatrix} 5 \\ 9 \\ -13 \end{pmatrix}$

D $\begin{pmatrix} 5 \\ 11 \\ -15 \end{pmatrix}$

2. A line l has equation $3y + 2x = 6$.

   What is the gradient of any line parallel to l?

   A $\quad -2$

   B $\quad -\dfrac{2}{3}$

   C $\quad \dfrac{3}{2}$

   D $\quad 2$

3. The diagram shows the graph of $y = f(x)$.

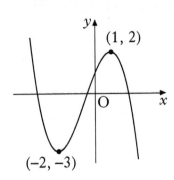

Which of the following shows the graph of $y = f(x + 2) - 1$?

A

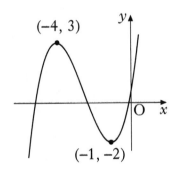

B

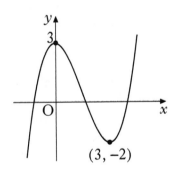

C

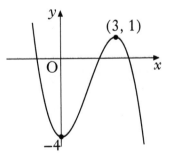

D

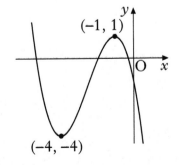

[Turn over

4. A tangent to the curve with equation $y = x^3 - 2x$ is drawn at the point (2, 4).

   What is the gradient of this tangent?

   A   2

   B   3

   C   4

   D   10

5. If $x^2 - 8x + 7$ is written in the form $(x - p)^2 + q$, what is the value of q?

   A   −9

   B   −1

   C   7

   D   23

6. The point P(2, −3) lies on the circle with centre C as shown.

   The gradient of CP is −2.

   What is the equation of the tangent at P?

   A $y + 3 = -2(x - 2)$

   B $y - 3 = -2(x + 2)$

   C $y + 3 = \frac{1}{2}(x - 2)$

   D $y - 3 = \frac{1}{2}(x + 2)$

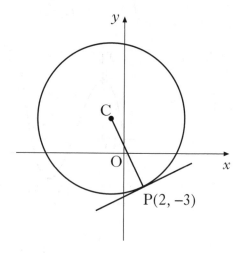

7. A function f is defined on the set of real numbers by $f(x) = x^3 - x^2 + x + 3$.

   What is the remainder when $f(x)$ is divided by $(x - 1)$?

   A   0

   B   2

   C   3

   D   4

8. A line makes an angle of 30° with the positive direction of the *x*-axis as shown.

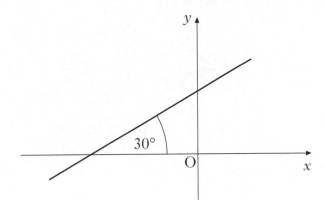

What is the gradient of the line?

A $\dfrac{1}{\sqrt{3}}$

B $\dfrac{1}{\sqrt{2}}$

C $\dfrac{1}{2}$

D $\dfrac{\sqrt{3}}{2}$

9. The discriminant of a quadratic equation is 23.

Here are two statements about this quadratic equation:

(1) the roots are real;

(2) the roots are rational.

Which of the following is true?

A   Neither statement is correct.

B   Only statement (1) is correct.

C   Only statement (2) is correct.

D   Both statements are correct.

[Turn over

FORMULAE LIST

Circle:

The equation $x^2 + y^2 + 2gx + 2fy + c = 0$ represents a circle centre $(-g, -f)$ and radius $\sqrt{g^2 + f^2 - c}$.

The equation $(x - a)^2 + (y - b)^2 = r^2$ represents a circle centre (a, b) and radius r.

Scalar Product: $\mathbf{a}.\mathbf{b} = |\mathbf{a}||\mathbf{b}| \cos \theta$, where θ is the angle between $\mathbf{a}$ and $\mathbf{b}$

or $\mathbf{a}.\mathbf{b} = a_1b_1 + a_2b_2 + a_3b_3$ where $\mathbf{a} = \begin{pmatrix} a_1 \\ a_2 \\ a_3 \end{pmatrix}$ and $\mathbf{b} = \begin{pmatrix} b_1 \\ b_2 \\ b_3 \end{pmatrix}$.

Trigonometric formulae:
$$\sin(A \pm B) = \sin A \cos B \pm \cos A \sin B$$
$$\cos(A \pm B) = \cos A \cos B \mp \sin A \sin B$$
$$\sin 2A = 2\sin A \cos A$$
$$\cos 2A = \cos^2 A - \sin^2 A$$
$$= 2\cos^2 A - 1$$
$$= 1 - 2\sin^2 A$$

Table of standard derivatives:

$f(x)$	$f'(x)$
$\sin ax$	$a \cos ax$
$\cos ax$	$-a \sin ax$

Table of standard integrals:

$f(x)$	$\int f(x)dx$
$\sin ax$	$-\frac{1}{a}\cos ax + C$
$\cos ax$	$\frac{1}{a}\sin ax + C$

[Turn over

SECTION A

ALL questions should be attempted.

1. A sequence is defined by the recurrence relation $u_{n+1} = 3u_n + 4$, with $u_0 = 1$.
   Find the value of u_2.

   A   7

   B   10

   C   25

   D   35

2. What is the gradient of the tangent to the curve with equation $y = x^3 - 6x + 1$ at the point where $x = -2$?

   A   −24

   B   3

   C   5

   D   6

3. If $x^2 - 6x + 14$ is written in the form $(x - p)^2 + q$, what is the value of q?

   A   −22

   B   5

   C   14

   D   50

4. What is the gradient of the line shown in the diagram?

   A $-\sqrt{3}$

   B $-\dfrac{1}{\sqrt{3}}$

   C $-\dfrac{1}{2}$

   D $-\dfrac{\sqrt{3}}{2}$

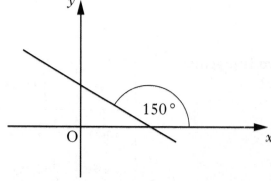

5. The diagram shows a right-angled triangle with sides and angles as marked.

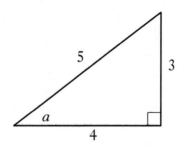

What is the value of cos2a?

A $\dfrac{7}{25}$

B $\dfrac{3}{5}$

C $\dfrac{24}{25}$

D $\dfrac{6}{5}$

6. If $y = 3x^{-2} + 2x^{\frac{3}{2}}$, $x > 0$, determine $\dfrac{dy}{dx}$.

A $-6x^{-3} + \dfrac{4}{5}x^{\frac{5}{2}}$

B $-3x^{-1} + 3x^{\frac{1}{2}}$

C $-6x^{-3} + 3x^{\frac{1}{2}}$

D $-3x^{-1} + \dfrac{4}{5}x^{\frac{5}{2}}$

7. If $\mathbf{u} = \begin{pmatrix} -3 \\ 1 \\ 2t \end{pmatrix}$ and $\mathbf{v} = \begin{pmatrix} 1 \\ t \\ -1 \end{pmatrix}$ are perpendicular, what is the value of t?

A -3

B -2

C $\dfrac{2}{3}$

D 1

[Turn over